MW00906141

The Loneliest Piano

Library and Archives Canada Cataloguing in Publication

Brott, Ardyth, 1951-
The loneliest piano / written by Ardyth Brott ; illustrated by Alena Skarina.

ISBN 978-1-77161-004-9

I. Skarina, Alena, 1986- II. Title.

PS8553.R682L66 2012 jC813'.54 C2012-907201-X

Mosaic Press gratefuly acknowledges the assistance of the Canada Book Fund, Department of Canadian Heritage, Government of Canada in support of our publishing program.

Pubished by Mosaic Press, Oakville, Ontario, Canada, 2014.
Distributed in the United States by Bookmasters (www.bookmasters.com).
Distributed in the U.K. by Gazelle Book Services (www.gazellebookservices.co.uk).

Designed by Eric Normann
ISBN 978-1-77161-004-9
ePub 978-1-77161-005-6
ePDF 978-1-77161-006-3

MOSAIC PRESS
1252 Speers Road, Units 1 & 2
Oakville, Ontario L6L 5N9

phone: (905) 825-2130
info@mosaic-press.com

www.mosaic-press.com

The Loneliest Piano

written by
Ardyth Brott

illustrated by
Alena Skarina

The book is dedicated to the memory of my father-in-law Alexander Brott, who inspired this story – A.B.

To my mother Tatiana Skarina who plays the piano every day for my dog and cats – A.S.

I was built by loving hands in Germany many years ago. I remember the craftsmen Fritz and Franz polishing my wood until it shone. They attached each string and wound it until it sang. I had so many wonderful notes. Eighty-eight in fact. Each one completely different. It was amazing!

Fritz & Frantz

Fritz and Franz hugged me as I was loaded onto the shiny red truck and waved good-bye with tears in their eyes. I was going far across the ocean to the busy city of New York, in America.

They knew I was going to a foreign land where few people spoke German and most people spoke English. I didn't care because everyone everywhere understood my musical language.

"Auf Wiedersehen!" yelled Fritz.

"Make beautiful music," cried Franz and he wiped away his tears with a very large handkerchief.

The journey across the Atlantic Ocean was horrible. I was loaded into the belly of a huge ship. It was dark and lonely and very scary.

MAIL
FRAGILE

There were smelly fish and even a few rats who tried to chew on my strings. The ship groaned a horrible bass sound as it lunged from side to side. It made me sea sick. I threw up several times on the harpsichord next to me.

The harpsichord refused to speak to me because I was only a piano.

There was no one there to hear me cry.

Finally the lurching stopped and an enormous crane unloaded me. I was frightened. I looked down and started to shake in mid air.

"Be careful ... don't let him swing," yelled the crane operator.

"He's a piano, he's supposed to swing," laughed the man on the dock.

I shook so hard my strings rattled and I thought my beautiful wood was going to split right off and fall into the water.

I was taken to a famous shop on 57th Street with lots of other pianos.

Everyone spoke different languages as they greeted the owners Lotte and Walter Schneckendorfer.

That first day I was lost and confused. But then at night, when the Schneckendorfers went home, something magical happened.

All the pianos
came to life.

"So what's your name?"
said Fifi the cute upright
piano to my left.

"I don't have a name ... no one ever gave me a name."

"Don't have a name? But this will not do. Everybody has to have a name. It's a rule. Why even violins and drums have names."

The concert grand named Basil yelled over. "We must give him a name, a special name. It has to be perfect."

"Let's see what he can do,
and then we'll decide,"
trilled Gertrude.

And so all night long we jammed. I'd never heard of jammin' before, but it sure was fun. They taught me how to Boogie-woogie, and do ragtime, and gospel songs and I showed off my concertos and I even played a Mozart duet with Fifi.

And at the end of the night they all announced, "his name will be Magnifico because he plays the best, the loudest, the most powerful chords of any piano in the shop."

I loved my new name.
It had such a nice
sound to it.

During the day, famous pianists would come and visit. Arthur Rubenstein played Chopin on me, Rudolf Serkin played Beethoven, Glenn Gould played Bach, Fats Waller and Billy Joel and Stevie Wonder played their own compositions! They would sit down at my bench and tickle my keys, and I would sing the most beautiful melodies.

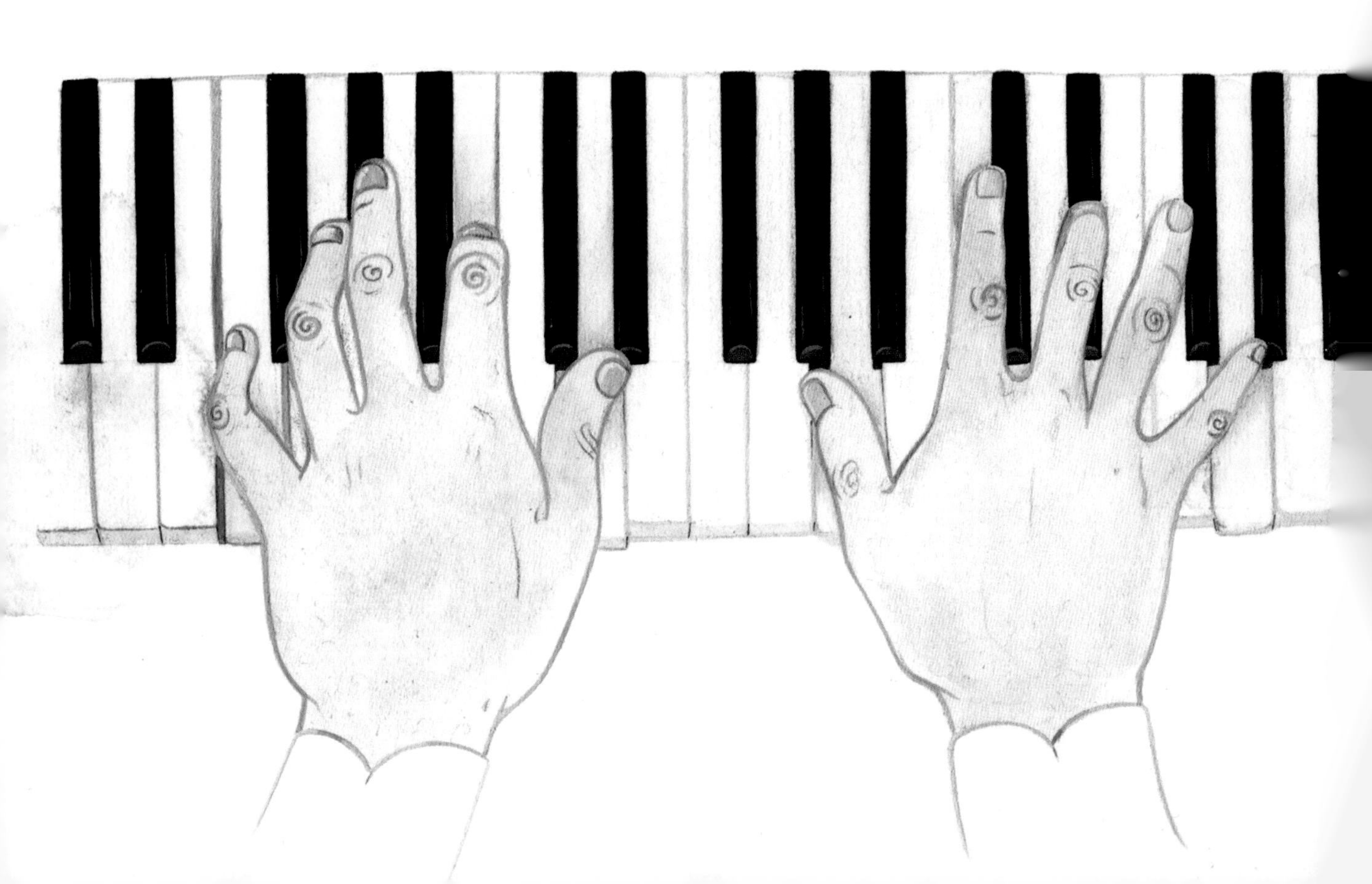

One day a very tall, bald man who smelled like garlic and sausages came to the Schneckendorfer's shop. He sat down and played on several pianos including me. Then I overheard him talking to Lotte about me and shipping me to Canada!

'Oh no,' I thought. 'More water, more boats, more rats' and I started to feel sick to my stomach.

I was kind of sad to say good bye to all my new friends at the piano shop. But that night they threw me a great good-bye party. We played Bach and Gershwin until the sun came up. My New York friends said I was a real hot piano and they would miss me.

Early the next morning, a big red truck appeared. Everyone waved good bye. I was kind of excited by my new adventure.

We arrived in Montreal on a cold February afternoon. The movers put a big blanket over me and huffed and puffed as they carried me up the winding staircase.

As the doors opened I heard the sounds of many different instruments coming from all the rooms.

All that music in one building. Life would be Grand!

But the truly marvelous part of the whole adventure was meeting my new owner, the Professor! He was a famous composer and had long hair and wore strange rocks hanging around his neck. The students said he was "cool" and an old "hippie".

I loved him. Sometimes, the Professor created new compositions with me. He took new melodies and harmonies from his head and played them on my keys. I felt so creative.

Then one day the big
red truck appeared.
We went for a
long drive
and I was
unloaded into
a beautiful
house by
the lake.

Unfortunately there were a lot of smelly fish but the view was great. I was given a place of honor in the living room with a huge ammonite sitting on my lid. At first I was a little scared of the ammonite, but now we have become friends.

As a matter of fact, without the ammonite, I would be the loneliest piano in the whole world.

Actually we are both very sad together. He tells me about his life in the Rocky Mountains 120 million years ago, and I tell him about my life with the old Professor and all his students.

You see, I have been in the house by the lake for 25 years. Mostly by myself. At first the Professor would come by from time to time. He hardly ever comes now.

I am the loneliest piano in the world.

For many years a little boy would come over. He liked to fish and his fingers smelled like Smallmouth bass and Sunfish and worms. He used to run in, flip back my lid, and play chopsticks on me. The same piece every time. The same 8 notes. He played chopsticks 2,147 times on me.

... then he moved away.

And now, every day I look out the window for the big red truck but the only person I ever see is a kind woman who comes and sprays furniture polish on me. She tries to be nice and sings songs to me but she doesn't know how to play the piano. And I hate furniture polish, it makes me cough and sneeze.

Sometimes she brings her cat who runs up and down my keys. But he's not a very musical cat and his pieces are not organized into patterns, and chords and harmonies. They're sort of jumping, splashing pieces if you know what I mean.

I look out over the lake which is now covered with snow. The spring birds are singing now. I dream of Fritz and Franz back in Germany and my old "jammin" friends in New York and I will never forget all those wonderful students. I can still remember the compositions created on my eighty eight keys.

But now I am silent and sad. How nice it would be to sing and laugh and play again. How I would love to play Scott Joplin and Bach, Chopin and Gershwin. If I had one single wish it would be to stop being a piece of furniture and to sing and jam again.

And then suddenly, the big red truck came. The men took me on a long truck ride. And then we stopped and the truck's doors opened and I saw the most beautiful sign I'd ever seen.

"STAGE DOORS"

Then I heard other pianos and violins and drums and clarinets and flutes and trumpets and piccolos and cellos and violas and trombones.

I looked up on the wall. There was another sign.

"CONCERT HALL"

I rattled my strings in my own secret happy song. Magnifico had finally come home.

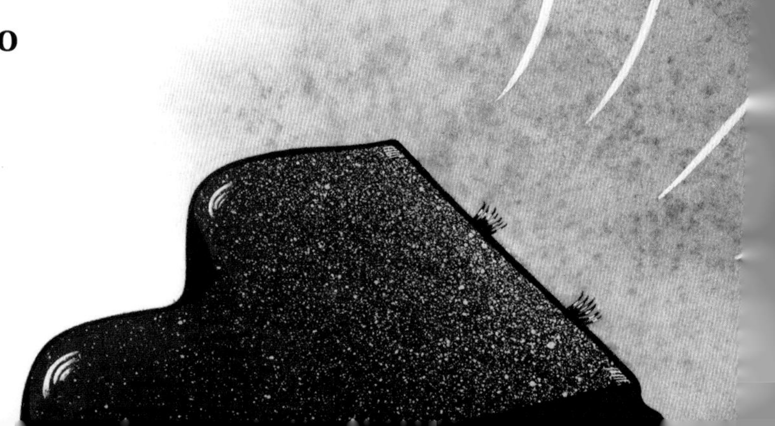

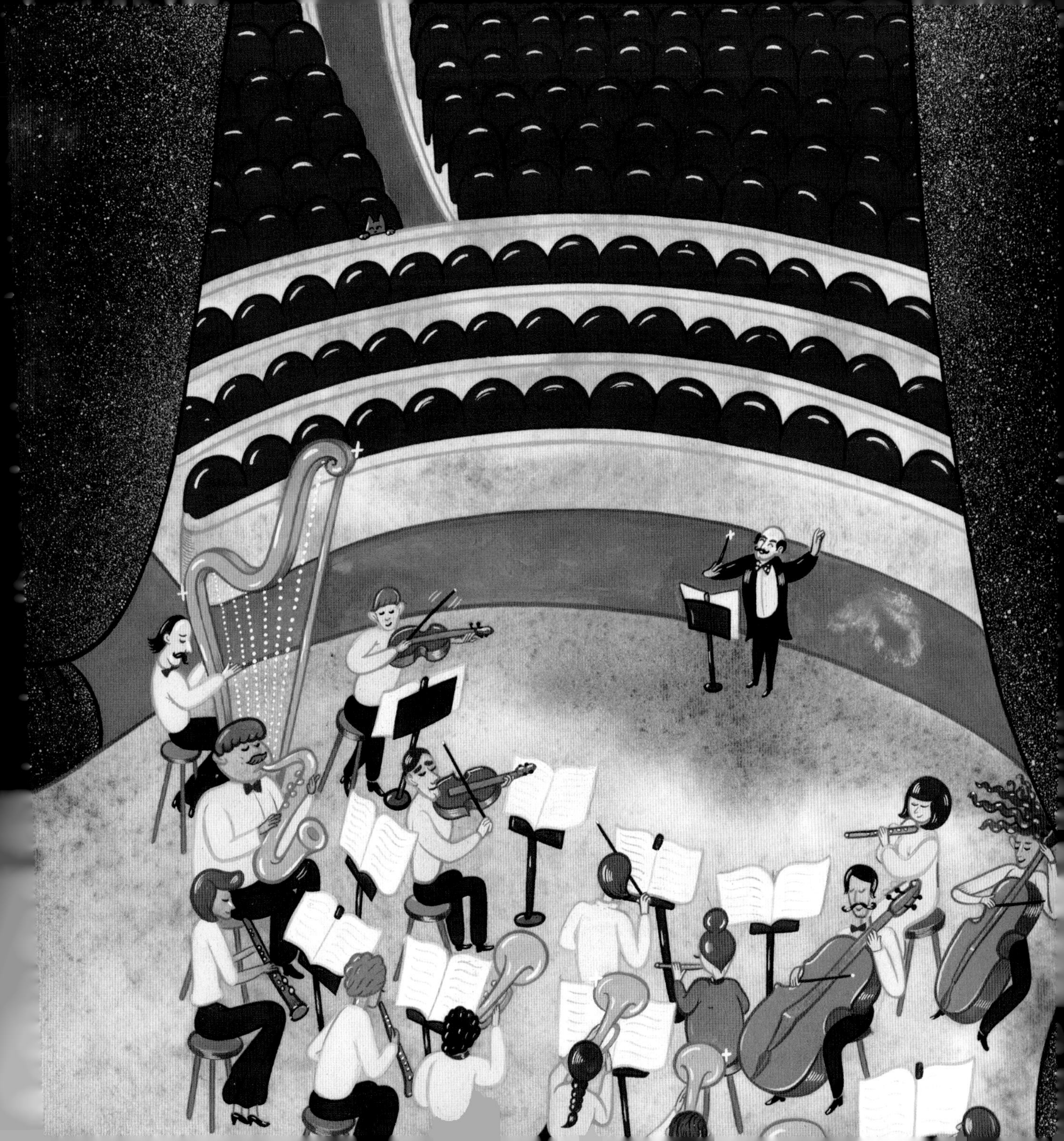

Fritz Frantz

Ardyth Brott is the author of the acclaimed children's books *Jeremy's Decision - Olivier Ne Sait Pas* and *HERE I AM!* She is also a lawyer and an arts administrator. She makes her home in Hamilton and Montreal.

Alëna Skarina is an award-winning illustrator and fine artist, born in Siberia, Russia in 1986. Alëna's visual education began at Protvino city Art School, Moscow Region, which she attended from the age of 7 to 12. After moving to Canada in 1999, she pursued a bachelor's degree in illustration, at the Ontario College of Art and Design. When Alëna was 17, she was picked up by a renowned Toronto-based illustration agency—Reactor Art & Design, who has been representing her ever since. The use of traditional mediums, refined line work and kind subject matter are integral elements in Alëna's work.

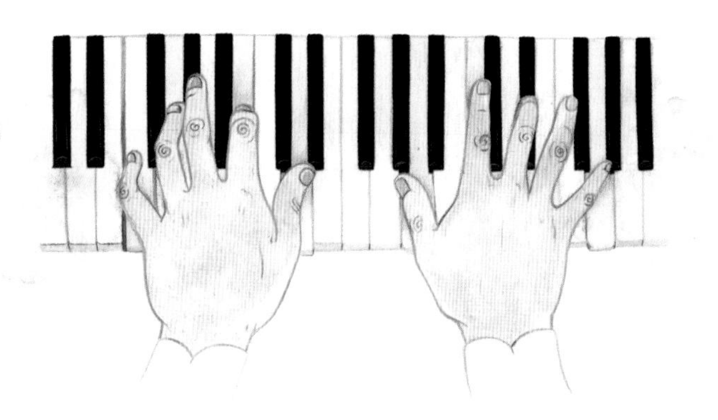